D1298434

The
Proteus Sails
Again:

Further Adventures
at the
End of the World

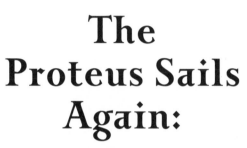

The Proteus Sails Again:

Further Adventures at the End of the World

Thomas M. Disch

SUBTERRANEAN PRESS 2008

First Edition

ISBN
978-1-59606-205-4

Subterranean Press
PO Box 190106
Burton, MI 48519

www.subterraneanpress.com

Invitation

Not, this time, an invocation. That is for the Muse, and it's like begging a favor. She has been there when I've needed her, and I remain grateful for that. But this is different—almost the opposite. This is like asking someone to come into your house. There is a whole class of people who would not be welcome without an invitation, or a search warrant. You have to ask them in before they can start visiting on a regular basis. Coleridge's faux ballad "Christabel" shows that rule in operation. The heroine of the title goes out in the forest one morning and meets a beautiful girl about her own age in great distress because she was just abducted by some horsemen and then taken far from home and abandoned. Her name is Geraldine. Naturally Christabel invites Geraldine to come to her own palace, which is conveniently nearby. And then

> They crossed the moat, and Christabel
> Took the key that fitted well
> A little door she opened straight
> All in the middle of the gate,
> The gate that was covered within
> > and without,
> Where an army in battle array
> > marched out.
> The lady [the evil Geraldine] sinks,
> > belike through pain,
> And Christabel with might and main
> Lifted her up, a weary weight,
> Over the threshold of the gate.
> Then the lady rose again,
> And moved, as she were not in pain.

Well, that was a mistake on Christabel's part. Geraldine turns out to be a kind of snake and also the daughter of her father's sworn enemy. Something awful seems about to happen—but Coleridge can't figure out what. The poem breaks off right there in a moment of maximum peril and mystery. But one thing has been made very clear. Don't invite strangers into your palace, no matter what kind of hard-luck story they tell you when you find them in the woods.

We never learn, do we? After all my experiences in ancient Greece, where things just as weird and creepy as anything in "Christabel" were a part of everyday life, I went and did the same dumb thing. I opened the door and shouted, "Okay, Trouble, come right in!"

I

Oh, and I should have thought to say you're invited, too. Yes, you, dear Reader. Don't be a weary weight, like Geraldine. Come in! And bring along the dog behind you in the hall. For all we know he might be Mephistofeles. That's how he makes his entrance, isn't it, in Goethe's *Faust*?

So we all went back into my apartment, I and my two invisible guests (the dog was a Lhasa apso and not just visible but very cute), where I plunked down in my blue recliner facing the defunct tv. Defunct except for playing DVDs: there'd been no cable service now since the bomb that wiped out Dubai. Why a bomb in Dubai would interfere with cable service in New York City has been a mystery to all of us, unless it is the simple ostrich cunning of any crowd when the cops drive by: we think if we are very quiet they won't know we're here. But cable service or no, I was not about to rearrange the furniture to suggest that my life had any other purpose than watching television. It didn't.

"Tom!" said a voice quite near at hand. "Hot damn, but it is so good to see you again. I've missed you. All your shipmates missed you, and Cassandra in particular. She says she feels all *abandonata*, like Dido in the opera."

"Oh, piss off," I said aloud. "You don't exist—you or the gentle reader beside you or that mangy mutt. You are all the fantasms of my wishful thinking. I am so used to hearing talking heads talking to me when I sit by this tv that it's become a habit. Next you'll be explaining the benefits of consolidating all my debts in one adjustable-rate mortgage."

"No, Tom. I think we've all learned our lesson with that one. Aren't you interested at all in knowing who I am?" (This was followed by a plaintive whine from the dog.)

"I know already. You're "No one"—as in the story of Ulysses in the cave of What's-His-Name."

"Polyphemus?" my reader suggested.

"In the cave of Polyphemus," I emended.

"You're being needlessly mean. I am *not* No one; I am someone you know very well. In fact, you murdered me."

My reader gasped. Apparently he had not yet got round to reading the first volume of this epic tale or he would have known that I am indeed a murderer, and he'd have had a fair suspicion that his fellow guest was the young sailor on the *Proteus* who'd challenged me to a contest of riddles and lost—both the contest and his life. That's how riddle contests worked in ancient Greece, and in ancient China, too, if we're to believe Puccini's *Turandot*.

But *what* was the fellow's name? For the life of me I couldn't remember.

That's when the phone rang. "Excuse me a moment," I told my guests and crossed the room to my desk, where the phone sat atop a metal loaf-pan so as to make its ring louder. My ears are not as young as they were.

As soon as I'd picked up and even before I could say hello, my friend Alice burst out, "Tom, oh thank heaven you're there. Where have you been, I've been trying to reach you all day. Is *Harry* there? I brought him by this morning and the *moment* we were out of the elevator he scooted down the hallway, the way he does, but when *I* got to your door he'd already gone inside, or that's what I assumed. But I knocked and knocked and you never came—"

"I was in Greece, "I explained, "with Agamemnon."

"Very funny, Tom, but this is serious. "When you didn't come, I called for Harry, but he'd simply vanished. He must have gone down those fire stairs, or up them, but I couldn't explore your whole building. When Harry wants to play hide-and-seek he can be *very* clever."

"In fact, Alice—" I reached down to chuck Harry under his fluffy beard. He was gazing up at the phone alertly as though it were Alice in person. Such a cutie. "In fact, Alice, he is with me right now. I don't know where he might have been earlier. He hasn't been to Greece with me, but he's here now."

"That's a great relief; I was so worried. Do give the little fellow something to eat and tell him one of your stories. You know how he loves to hear you rattle on. I'll come by later to get him, but I can't really say when because the Queen is coming by any minute and I have to finish making the crumpets."

"The Queen?" (Thinking this must be some kind of coded reference I wasn't picking up on.)

"If you can go camping with Agamemnon, I should be allowed a few moments with the Queen. Oh, and a bowl of water. Harry gets terribly thirsty in this wretched heat." With which she hung up.

Harry tilted his head sideways, as though to say, "Isn't she something."

II

"By the way, Mr. Disch," said my reader in a tentative tone, "I *am* real. You might not have been able to see me the *moment* I came in the door, but after a bit I'll solidify. It's like when you boot up your computer; it takes a while. I don't know if it's the same for your other friend."

"Can *you* see him?"

"No, I gather he's a ghost. I'm more of a fantasm, or an apparition. There are different rules for different paranormal entities. Some *delusions* are never visible. They're strictly auditory."

"Oh, I'm visible, mate," said a voice from the other side of the room. "If you want to see me all you have to do is turn on the tv.

"I'll do that," I assured him, "but first things first. Harry needs something to eat. And a bowl of water." I foraged through the refrigerator and found an opened can of Broadcast corn beef hash that had grown a film of mold while I'd been off in ancient Greece, but I scraped off the mold and it smelled okay, and Harry, after one inquiring sniff, didn't raise any objection. Then I filled the second largest of the nesting crystal bowls with water from the tap.

Then I found the remote and turned on the tv.

As soon as I saw his face, I remembered his name: Socrates. But how incredibly he'd aged since I had answered his riddle and had to kill him. He'd been no more than a teenager then with the first wisps of a peach-fuzz beard. Now he was a middle-aged man.

If his flesh had been marble he'd have looked just like a traditional bust of his namesake, the philosopher. This Socrates, however, had very bad skin, pitted and pocked and splotchy and hatched with scars like the faces of most older Greek men of his day and age, who were in the habit of attacking each other with knives and swords. Indeed, there was a long red seam across his throat just where sailors and convicts of a more recent era would have a dotted line and "Cut Here" tattooed, a souvenir of our last encounter in the flesh.

"To what do I owe this honor?" I asked him.

He looked up brightly with the special pathos of a wasted con who still has an ingenuous teenager immured within, like a seed that's never sprouted. "Hey, Tom, you are my main man, you know that. I have been trying to get hold of you for centuries, literally. I have been born again and born again, over and over. Cassandra taught me all about reincarnation. Every time I'm born again I set off to sea. Lord Poseidon, the ships I've been on! I'm like that guy in the Wagner opera, except that *he* was a captain, and I've never been anything but a lob-scouser. That's slang for sailor. From the nineteenth century. I've sailed with Nelson. With Melville. Sucked his cock, too."

His voice was getting very faint, and his image was fading so that I could see the talk-show set through his ectoplasmic face. "Socrates," I told him, "you're fading."

"I can't help that, Tom. It's part of being a ghost. But I know what you can do that'll fix it. It's the same as what Ulysses did when he wanted to perk up his old mom when he went down to hell and *she* wouldn't talk. Some blood. It works even better than wine, though I wouldn't mind some of that either. But you've got that little machine you use every morning. I've watched you jab your finger with it."

"It tests my blood-sugar level. I have diabetes."

"Whatever. Give your finger a prick and squeeze out a good glob of the red stuff and kind of smoosh it across the screen."

It seemed little enough to ask, so I drew a droplet of blood from my middle finger and swiped it across the tv screen. Socrates grinned and leaned forward with his tongue out, mutt-like. From inside the tv he licked away the blood on the outside of the screen, and with each thirsty pass of his tongue, his image became brighter and clearer. Then, suddenly, he wasn't there in the tv studio, and he wasn't inside the tv. He was sitting in the other recliner in the room in an outfit that looked like he'd picked it up at a Goodwill fire sale—white polyester pants frayed at the cuff and stained yellow at the crotch and a tee-shirt advertising Copenhagen snuff. In high-definition reality his bad skin looked even worse. He was charming and repugnant in about equal measure.

"I don't understand any of this," said my reader, who was standing beside the chair Socrates was sitting in.

"Socrates," I said, "would you fill him in? I have a sudden urgent need to get to the bathroom. Excuse me."

Harry gave one crisp bark to explain that he would accompany me to the john and we left the room together.

III

Learning a foreign language is, for most of us, the most difficult task we will ever accomplish.

For Americans it seems even a little harder than for other peoples. Perhaps because, these days, there is such a great expanse of the country that is monoglot, where one never hears a discouraging (i.e. foreign) word; perhaps because we're all a bunch of racist bigots as the zealots of the Reconquesta maintain; perhaps because the one foreign language we are likely to have tried our tongues at has lately been such a bone of contention. Should Spanish become the *official* language of California, Nevada, and New Mexico, as the voters of those states have recently decided? That may be a neat quid pro quo for all the other states where English has been accorded a similar primacy, but it has led to some nasty riots, forest fires, and other kinds of civil broils.

It must be admitted that language can be a tool of oppression. The Arabs were canny to make the memorization of the Koran the basis of education in all their conquered territories, setting generations of boys the task of memorizing the whole Holy Writ, whether or not they understood a word of it. Talk about submission! Or how about those Norsemen? After they had been put to the trouble of learning French and good table manners in their new-christened "Normandy" they went to England and lorded it over the Saxons for centuries. To this day a "good accent" counts for as much as clean fingernails.

But there is another, sweeter side to language acquisition: one falls in love. Not just with the language but with a Significant Autre who embodies the beauty, wisdom, finesse, and brio of the language one desires to learn. Years ago I sold Harper & Row a schema for developing a series of computer-interactive educational "games" called "Foreign Affairs," in which the player would learn French, German, and Italian (the three languages in which I had proven my own incompetence) by falling in love with a virtual bon ami, liebling, or inamorata and learning the loved one's language by the time-honored means of whispering sweet nothings to each other. What is this? This is a nose! What is this? And so on. Alas, Harper & Row discontinued their software department before "Foreign Affairs" got off the ground and while my first contracted-for computer-interactive game, *Amnesia*, was still only half written and programmed.

(H & R still hasn't gone completely bankrupt, but Cassandra tells me that day is fast approaching, now that Murdoch has deaccessioned the imprint to a Chinese publishing conglomerate specializing in magazines about pro wrestling and astrology. *Plus ça change*, as the French say.)

But I digress. I set out to speak of Socrates and the linguistic competence he had acquired over the course of his centuries as *un matelot maudit* doomed to roll around on the bounding main. Apart from the Greek he was born with, with its many dialects and pidgins, he had a working knowledge of Phoenician, Latin, Arabic, Spanish, Danish, Dutch, and English, all acquired in the old-fashioned What-is-this-this-is-a-nose way described above. Seamen have got lots of time on their hands when they are not swabbing decks or mending nets, and they put it to use by whittling scrimshaw and conjugating irregular verbs and coiffing each other's hair. For anyone of a naturally phlegmatic temperament it is a sweet life.

"What is that?" Socrates had crossed the room to stand before the window looking down at the upper end of Union Square. "Is that 9-11?"

"Oh no," I said, not bothering to get up. "9-11 is much bigger than that. And it's a lake now. Or a lagoon. Footprint Lagoon some people call it. There are daredevils who go swimming there, but I'm told there are treacherous undercurrents and eddies, so the people who go swimming are often drowned as well."

"Then what is *that?*" Socrates insisted.

"That is, or was, a McDonald's."

"McDonald's the hamburger?"

"Precisely. Though as you can see now it is just a bomb crater. Nationally it was the forty-seventh to be bombed. At that point in time. By now there are well over two hundred. But this is the only one in New York City. Security *is* tight here."

"Why don't they rebuild it?" my reader asked in a tone of irritation. "It look terrible like that. And people have thrown their garbage down there. There are rats! Very many rats."

"Oh, there are rats all over the place these days, not just in the bomb craters. And it's only from up here that it seems so unsightly. At street level there is an attractive red-and-gold plywood barricade that says Reopening Soon! Of course it won't. Once PETA has bombed a place it stays bombed. Even without that threat hanging over it, I doubt that any McDonald's anywhere is going to be opening *or* re-opening any time soon. The customers aren't there. They're afraid of PETA. Of ALF, of ELF, of every schoolgirl in the country who wants to save the planet and the rainforests by bombing carnivores and liberating sneakers from the wreckage. Terrorism has become the new year-round carnival."

"Mr. Disch, really!" said my reader. "It's *not* as bad as all that. As the President has said, 'This too shall pass.' And it doesn't help things to just complain and complain. It isn't the end of the world."

"That's debatable."

"You wouldn't have a gun, would you?" Socrates asked. "It's might be fun to shoot the rats."

"Sorry, Old Soc. Guns aren't legal in the city."

IV

I doze a lot. I didn't use to, but these days I sit down in that blue recliner, tilt it back and I'm off. To Dreamland? Or to ancient Greece? Who's to say? It certainly sounds like the easy way out for a writer who wants to travel through time. And the Greece I get to in my easy chair is scarcely the Greece of Thucydides or even Mary Renault (whom I venerate). My Greece has to be accounted at least as mythical as Robert Graves'. And yet.

And yet I did bring home a genuine Bronze Age artifact, and any time I want a boing of Believe-It-or-Not bewilderment I only have to reach across my desktop to where the riddle knife sits, transformed into a mere letter opener, but with the same keen edge that sliced open Socrates' throat when he was a mere lad of fifteen and a sailor aboard the *Proteus*. But that will have to do for exposition. The thing is: how did I get hold of such an artifact if I hadn't really traveled back to 1100 BC or whenever it was the Trojan War came to an end?

I'd been asleep, and now I was awake and could see I had not been the only sleeper for there at my feet was Harry, a warm oval of butterscotch-colored fur, eyes closed, black nose atwitch to show he was having his own dream. Probably not set in the Aegean, but who knows what dogs dream of and what kinds of budgets their dreams command? He'd been adopted from a shelter. Perhaps he was the canine equivalent of royalty, abducted from his royal kennel and then left to his fate in a city where his royalty offered no advantage. Also curled up on another part of the carpet was my reader, whose name I still did not know. He was a man of middle years and dressed, like myself, right out of Land's End catalogue. In fact, we were wearing the same pair of soft violet ("periwinkle" my niece Sara called them) corduroy slacks, which had been reduced to just $19.95 in the last Land's End Clearance catalogue. I wonder if he'd also sprung for the Harvest Orange trousers at the same low price. Cheapskates always end up sporting those colors no one ever buys at full price.

But Socrates was not to be seen.

"Socrates?"

"I'm here, Tom. I'm sitting on the rug right in front of you. But I guess I'm fading again. How long has it been since you let me lick the blood off your tv?"

"I don't know. I think I fell asleep."

"And you are my main man. When you sleep I kind of fade. Can you hear me okay?"

I nodded, squinting at the dust motes jittering in the rays of afternoon sunlight as though he might materialize among them, or at least some follow-the-dots approximation.

"If I had some blood again.... I don't want to seem like a vampire."

"Oh certainly." I looked about for my blood-sugar testing device.

"I'll get it," said Socrates. There were footsteps, a rustling sound, and then without visible support the bronze riddle knife floated across the room toward me. I felt peculiar pricking my finger with the same knife I'd used to murder the fellow, but I'm a lazy fellow and didn't insist on getting my diabetes kit. A prick, a pinch, and then I held out my finger for Socrates to have his ration of blood.

He re-materialized before me, licking his lips appreciatively.

Harry barked.

"You, too?" I pinched out another droplet of blood and offered my finger to Harry. But that was not what he was after. He needed to take a piss.

V

"**Y**ou know what my favorite book is?" Socrates asked the next morning, after a breakfast of Pepsi-Cola and Twinkies, which he'd bought himself at what had been a news kiosk staffed by illegal aliens in burqas. (There are no supermarkets these days, not since the first food riots.)

"I wouldn't have thought you *had* a favorite book," I replied, not looking up from the Drudge Report. I found it difficult to talk with someone who was standing on his head.

"*On the Road.* I've never actually read it, but you don't to read a lot of books to have a favorite. I like the idea that's behind it. It's so American."

"Which is?" my reader asked, echoing my tone of Mensa-like hauteur. (I've never been a member, but sometimes I have that air.)

"Which is, like, Drive!" Socrates flipped upright in a single abrupt motion, then pantomimed his idea of steering a race car, complete with sound effects. Harry got caught up in the excitement and barked encouragingly.

"But you know what I don't understand?" The race car slowed thoughtfully. "Why don't *you* have a car, Tom? You're an American."

"Actually I do have a car, a Dodge Caravan. But it's in the country, and its battery is probably dead."

"That's too bad. Because if it were *here*, we could all pile in and drive to California. Cassandra would have loved California. The women have real watermelon boobs there, right? I love the Mamas and the Papas. I was on this tanker going round the Horn and we played the Mamas and the Papas non-stop. She would have fit right in."

"Cassandra did not have 'watermelon' boobs! She had ideal breasts. The breasts of a Venus de Milo."

"You never ask about her," Socrates observed. "Aren't you curious what became of her?"

He put his hands in place on the carpet and levered himself upside-down again. He insisted that half-an-hour a day in a hand-stand was the secret of cardiovascular health. Who was I to gainsay that? He'd been alive, or at least undead, for centuries.

"Well," I replied in my tone of thought-ful, benign superiority, "I already *know* what became of the poor woman. It's a tragic tale, one of the most famous. There have been operas about it. But as for having all the gory details filled in, thanks but no thanks."

"Well, *I'm* curious," my reader volun-teered. "How *did* she die?"

"She didn't. In fact, she and Agamemnon and most of your old shipmates are all here in New York. We got here on the *Proteus*, which is docked at this moment on Staten Island."

"No way," said my reader.

"Way," said Socrates. "And I'll tell you how."

VI

This is the story Socrates told.

There had been dissensions among Agamemnon's officers as to the division of spoils—not just what had been plundered from Troy but also from the coastal cities and islands of the Aegean. Quite a lot of desirable items had been amassed, and no one desired them more avidly than Agamemnon's second-in-command, Neoptolemus. Chief among those items was a Persian slave girl, Lamia. No on-shore gathering of the fleet was complete without a performance by Lamia and her seven snakes. How anyone is able to train snakes to accomplish such prodigies was a secret known only to Lamia and the women of her guild somewhere in central Persia. At last, after much whining and wheedling by Neoptolemus (and remembering what trouble had been caused by similar disagreements with the fellow's father Achilles), Agamemnon had given him the girl. Now it was *his* turn to sulk in his tent.

Cassandra was not without wiles. She saw in this quarrel an opportunity to trick Agamemnon into saving his own ass—and hers—while avenging himself on his grasping subaltern. Agamemnon confided to the young captain that he had become so besotted with his Trojan slave, the mad Cassandra, that he could not bear the thought of being parted from her. He knew that the moment they debarked in Argos, Clytemnestra would realize that she had a rival in Cassandra, whose ravings were not so incoherent as to be opaque. Even aboard the ship she hurled taunts and insults at his wife. Surely in Argos she would try to queen it over Clytemnestra still more brazenly. It did not take prophetic powers to foresee unhappy consequences.

What if (Agamemnon suggested to Neoptolemus) the younger man were to assume the armor and lordly manner of Agamemnon and present himself to the Argives as the conquering hero returned? He'd been abroad more than ten years. Discretely disguised—a bandage about his jaw, a patch over one eye—Clytemnestra could be conned into believing what all his attendant soldiers seemed to affirm, that the imposter was her husband. A husband who would enjoy the rights and pleasure of a king, including the easy enjoyment of the captive Trojan women (i.e. Lamia, who would be exhibited in chains as the princess Cassandra).

With Neoptolemus ensconced on the throne of Argos, Agamemnon would be free to cruise the wine-dark Mediterranean with the madwoman he adored, free to lead the life of a freebooter unburdened by kingly care. He would need only the *Proteus*, its crew, and a reasonable share of his booty. Those captains who wished to might accompany the *Proteus* on its extended voyage, while those whose ardor for Poseidon's realm had cooled might go ashore with Neoptolemus.

"And you would surrender your crown just to run off with this—ruined woman?" Neoptolemus had marveled.

"I would consider myself blessed by the gods."

Neoptolemus had taken the bait, and the rest is to be read in the works of the Greek dramatists, most especially in Aeschylus' masterpiece, the *Oresteia*. While Clytemnestra may have suspected that the man she would butcher in his bathtub was an imposter, it scarcely mattered. He had been garlanded with the bays of victory by a cheering multitude assembled before his throne. Once he was slain there'd be a funeral pyre. Who could say the resulting ashes were not those of Agamemnon? Clytemnestra would rule Argos as queen—as she had been doing, in effect, for years.

As for poor Lamia, in the role of the subjugated Cassandra, she would die in the general slaughter of Agamemnonites. Raving, indeed, as Cassandra so famously raved, but raving in her native Persian. No one would understand a word of what she was trying to say. No whistle-blower she.

VI

"Pretty clever, wouldn't you say?" Socrates declared, concluding his tale. "That Cassandra is one wily woman."

"It is not unlike the Greeks' trick with that wooden horse," commented my reader.

"Right," Socrates agreed. "Only different. This time it was the Greeks who got killed. And it was a bloody massacre, let me tell you. I saw the whole damn thing from what you could say was a ringside seat. Ghosts have that advantage."

"You alone survived to tell the tale, as one might say," my reader quipped, thinking to lob his reference over Socrates' head.

Who just smiled with nostalgic satisfaction for the slaughter he'd witnessed so long ago. Which, having witnessed, he had reported back to the real Agamemnon and Cassandra aboard the *Proteus* and received, as his reward, gallons of blood from a bull held in reserve to celebrate the occasion. So much blood, indeed, that he nearly OD'ed. Though that embellishment was probably his idea of a joke. Socrates had become a kind of sophisticate of proletarian decadence over the centuries. He could tell you just what taverns in the Harlem of Franz Hals were best for scoring knockout hash, which streets to cruise in pre-Hannibalite Carthage for the most abject and obliging street urchins, where to get the best prices for rings, swords, furs, silverware and even silk snotrags in any major port on the North Atlantic. Yet pose a question about the politics or literature of the eras he'd passed through, and he was clueless. The

Socrateses of our own time are not much different except insofar as some of them will echo the opinions of a Rush Limbaugh or an Al Sharpton. Which is, in its way, a broadening of their horizons if not an elevation of their taste.

Still, you really can't be choosy in the matter of one's supernatural confidants. You take what you get. Rilke had his angels, Keats his nightingales, and I had Socrates. I asked him whatever had become of my old blood-brother Homer, and he assured me he was still on board the *Proteus* where it was docked, invisibly, in the shadow of the Verrazano Narrows Bridge. After the Iliad and the Odyssey he'd written many more epic poems, but all the amanuenses to whom they'd been dictated had in the course of time jumped ship and taken his manuscripts with them. Now he lived a reclusive existence to the degree that that can be done on board ship. Of course, it was no longer exactly the same ship it had been thirty centuries ago. It had been overhauled and patched up and redecorated , and now it was working as a ferryboat going back and forth from Staten Island to hell. But all that in its proper place.

Socrates had only begun to give his account of the many voyages of the *Proteus* (or the *Port Sue*, or the *E.S. Troup*, or the other names it had been registered under), when we were interrupted by Harry, who was in a state of high alarm and trying to explain, by his barking, what we had to do. Now! This instant! Stop talking! Follow me! He was just like Lassie when she is trying to alert the slow-witted people on her program that trouble is afoot.

So we followed him out into the hallway (someone had left the door open) and down the back fire stairs to the tenth floor, where the door to the apartment just beneath mine was wide open. The apartment of the actress

Elizabeth Ashley, who, back in 1999, had destroyed our apartment, and wrecked both Charlie's life and mine, when a lit cigarette she'd thrown into her trash can had started what became a five-alarm fire. All my papers, my clothes, half my library, all Charlie's papers and CDs, our furniture, years of tchotchkes, houseplants, paintings—gone. What the fire didn't destroy, the fire hoses finished off.

Ashley herself left her apartment right after she had set the fire. When she returned the fire trucks were already on the job. She still lives in the apartment below, but never in all the time since the fire did she ever apologize to either of us, though we often passed each other in the lobby. Not once an "I'm sorry." All of which might well be accounted a motive for murder.

But I swear by all the gods of Olympus *I* did not do the deed. Yet there she was, in a cheap flannel nightgown soaked with blood on the floor of her entrance hall, eyes staring, stabbed repeatedly in her chest and neck. Blood still was seeping from the wounds, most copiously where the murder weapon was still lodged just below her heart. And the weapon was one I recognized at once, for I had used it in centuries past to murder the man—the ghost, rather—standing beside me.

"Holy hell," said Socrates. "That's *my* knife!"

"It looks like it's hers now," said my reader.

Harry barked a single yip of I-told-you-so satisfaction. He knew that if ever a good dog there was, it was him. He'd sniffed out trouble and led us to its source. Lassie herself could have done no more.

The stain was still spreading across the flannel's floral print, turning all the little white and pink daisies a uniform lurid scarlet.

I had to think: what to do.

Socrates was having the same thought, and he had his answer already. "Hey mate, if you wouldn't mind…?" He nudged at my knee with his right foot, and with un-thinking complicity I stood and took up Harry in my arms lest he get Elizabeth's blood on his butterscotch-colored fur. His front paws were already dabbled.

Socrates knelt beside the corpse and tugged out the riddle knife from where it was embedded in her breast. Then, as fresh blood welled from the wound, he pressed his lips against that source of primal pleasure. He sucked up the blood as long as it continued to flow.

My reader, myself and the dog all watched with varying degrees of squeamish-ness and envy.

What to do, what to do. I realized I would be a suspect. The long-ago fire was still a good motive. The weapon, somehow, had come from my desk. And in terms of an alibi my only witnesses were two incorporeal spirits and a lhasa apso.

"Okay!" said Socrates, licking his lips with satisfaction and getting to his feet with the air of a man ten years younger than the one I'd just been talking to in my apartment minutes earlier. Blood will do that for a ghost. "We got ourselfs a murder mystery here. And I know just the person who can solve it."

"Cassandra! Of course!"

"You said it, Mate. The lady's a python-ess. And a murderess herself, come to that. And hey, you're another. And so am I." He looked at my reader with an inquisitive tilt of his head.

My reader shook his head. "No, I've always been an innocent bystander."

"So you say. But in a good mystery that would make you Suspect Number One. Anyhow you definitely qualify as a witness. So you come along too. We're heading to

Staten Island and the *U.S. Trope*. That's the name the *Proteus* goes by now. It has all the same letters but they've been rearranged."

"Ah ha," said my reader, ever alert to some hidden significance. "An anagram!"

VII

We were back upstairs in my apartment.

"That knot is never gonna hold," Socrates declared with a Jack Tar disdain of all lubbers. "Here, give it to me."

I handed him the length of twine from which I'd been fashioning a leash by which to lead Harry home to Alice.

"And what a wretched excuse for rope this is. Oh well." He scootched down beside the dog and set to work. Harry was twitchy. He had a canine prejudice against ghosts, even one as friendly as Socrates.

"I didn't know you had a dog," said my

reader, already waiting at the door "I know you have a thing for teddy bears. You've done two whole books about them. But you never mentioned a dog."

"I don't. This is Alice's dog. My friend Alice."

"He *acts* like your dog," said Socrates. "There!" He handed me the other end of the twine, and at once the knot he'd tied about the collar fell limp as though he'd tied no knot at all. "Damn. It does that sometimes. Material, immaterial, which is which, son of a bitch."

Harry barked, as though to say, "I win!"

While I tried my hand again, Socrates scratched his crotch (he had fleas, he claimed, that had been with him for centuries) and went on complaining. "I will stick something in my pocket, money someone's left on a table at a restaurant, a set of car keys, whatever, and when I reach for it later, it's gone. Damnedest thing."

"It's not the best twine, I'll admit. I just can't think of what else will serve the purpose. Harry, hold still! I got it for bundling up the newspapers. Some of the other tenants on the floor just set out a loose stack by the freight elevator, but I always made a neat bundle. But now I don't get the *Times* any more so I have all this twine."

"You don't get the *Times?*" my reader marveled.

"Not since the price went up to a dollar and a quarter. And at the same time it shrank in size. Plus, any news that's really news is there on the Drudge Report or on CNN, and hours sooner. And the kiosk by the park sells sodas and Twinkies now instead of newspapers. The one thing I've missed is the daily crossword. And every other Sunday, the Double-crostic. But for ten-fifty every week? And what I've discovered is that when you don't read the news it stops happening. Who cares who'll run for

President four years from now? Or which city has become the new Atlantis? It was sad to see Venice disappear. But Gdansk? Calcutta?

"Tragedies, sure. But I've got my own tragedies." I got to my feet and tugged at the makeshift leash. My knot held, and Harry growled and then yielded to his fate.

"That's true for all of us, mate," said Socrates, as he followed us out of the apartment and waited for me to lock the door. "Carthage? You should have seen the place when the Romans were done with it. And there weren't newspapers back then, or tv, or any of that, so when the *Proteus* approached we didn't know why it wasn't there any more. Like you say, tragic. When I think of all those kids around the docks and warehouses. Hundreds! They didn't care if you was a ghost or a leper or what. Like Homer said, they would give you a blow job just for the sake of your cum, they was that hungry."

"Homer *joined* you on your expedition?" my reader asked, aghast.

"Hey, just because the guy is blind doesn't mean he's a eunuch."

By this point we were inside the elevator and heading down to the first floor. We were fortunate in living in a building in which our landlords—Aristotle Ellis and his two sisters—also had their residence. It meant that such amenities as the elevators and security were not stinted.

What it also meant became evident when the elevator stopped at the ninth floor and Pooja, one of the aforesaid sisters, was revealed standing before the opened elevator door with her gigantic Irish wolfhound that was the terror of all the residents. Which was what we called him, Terror.

Pooja was no less striking and in a similar way. She seemed one of that new breed of fashion models, very tall, very thin, and with an air of active menace. She must have spent hours every day painting a demon mask on a face by nature hawk-like—with thin red lips, eyebrows like two poison darts, and pale bruised cheeks to either side of a beaky nose. She must have decided in her teenage years—not that long ago—that since she would never be beautiful she would instead be hideous.

At first sight of the two of them, Harry barked his claim of ownership. Terror barked back, with so much greater authority that even Harry was daunted. He backed up to stand behind my cane, and Pooja and her Terror entered the elevator cage, she with her usual sneer of a smile, Terror with a scythe-like motion of his tail, a motion that sliced right through my reader's crotch. He winked out of existence.

Terror looked down at little Harry in much the way that the T-Rex in *Jurassic Park* studied the small mammals in the hotel kitchen. Harry, ever the courtier, sniffed at

Terror's paws by way of showing his defer-
ence. Pooja tilted back her eagle beak to
show she took no notice of low creatures like
Harry, but I leaned forward to look more
closely. Once again Harry was showing
himself to be an astute detective. Could it be
blood that had stained Terror's large, leonine
paws as it had Harry's? The blood of
Elizabeth Ashley? Pooja did not have the
demeanor of someone who'd stumbled
upon the body of a murder victim. But then
neither (I hoped) did I.

Terror produced a low growl that told
Harry to mind his own business. He did not
have to be told twice but turned his attention to the rubber tip of my cane.

When we reached the first floor and
Pooja and her familiar had exited the elevator I held the door open to allow my reader
time to rematerialize and follow Socrates
into the marble hallway. Harry peeked
around the open door to make sure the coast

was clear, and then all four of us headed for the door to the street.

Until I remembered: it was after four. The mail should have arrived. I signaled a pause, fumbled in my pocket for the ring of keys, fit the smallest of them into the lock, and reached inside my own little pigeonhole to discover: yet another bill for *Interview* magazine insisting that I pay for the year's subscription I had neither ordered nor ever received; a book of discount coupons to our defunct McDonald's; the Con Ed bill; and—"Just a moment, guys. I've got to look at this."

It was a letter from my lawyer... The State Supreme Court court had overturned Judge Milan's decision of last August. The eviction process would begin again.

"Are you okay, Mr. Disch?" my reader asked.

"I'm fine," I assured him with my bravest smile.

"What was in the letter? You seem upset."

"It was my death warrant," I said, smiling still more bravely, and fainted dead away.

VIII

"**D**id I blank out again?" I asked when I came to in the front seat of the taxi that Socrates was driving *very* slowly down Fifth Avenue. "I'm sorry. I do that all the time these days. Sometimes for no reason at all."

"But this time, I take it, there was a reason?" my reader asked. "Something that was in that letter?" He was sitting in the back seat with Harry in his lap.

I figured that was none of his business, and asked, myself, of Socrates: "Where did this taxi come from?"

"It was parked along the curb. Finders keepers. That's an old Greek saying."

"Grand theft auto. That's an American saying."

"Have you ever played that game?" my reader asked me.

In reply Socrates made a squealing sound and made the taxi zig-zag, throwing a scare into one of the few pedestrians on the street. There was also very little traffic anywhere on Fifth Avenue. Maybe there had been another terror alert, although I hadn't heard any sirens.

"That game," Socrates declared, "is how I *learned* to drive. Vehicular homicide is my middle name."

"And 'hick' for short?" More and more it seemed to me that my reader was not a nice person. I hope all his gratuitous put-downs were not a habit he'd picked up from me. But that was not a subject I was not about to raise in front of his most recent target. So I changed the subject: "Socrates, do you know where you're taking us?"

"Our destiny?"

"Our destination," my reader corrected, then answered the question himself: "We are going to your friend Alice's apartment to return her dog to her. Her address is on Harry's collar, and I know Manhattan well enough to map our course, which is straight down Fifth, till we hit the park, then left till we come to the end of Macdougal."

"But hey," said Socrates, "our *destiny*'s another matter. If you want a taste of that, just grab hold of my cock."

"Oh, Socrates, you are impossible."

"Seriously, dude. Remember when you and Cassandra were going at it back on the ship. All the stuff she could see in your head? Well, there's a whole side of reality *you* don't connect with unless your cock's plugged in the socket. So to speak. Just grab hold and look out the window."

Curiosity is my ruling vice, so I slid my hand inside his grimy polyester bellbottoms, and there before us, and all about the cab, was indeed a sight to behold—crowds, throngs, torrents of people, pushing and shoving and clawing at the windows of the cab, clamorous with their demands—to have us open the windows, to be let in, to be given food, water, wine, blood, their god-damn, god-given rights. They were dressed in rags of all nations as though for a Fourth of July parade through hell. From time to time, slowly and carefully though he steered through the mob, Socrates would collide with one of them and, just as in an arcade game, a gong would sound and a yellow light would strobe and the whole excited mass of them would disappear. Then like a tv screen adjusting itself they'd return en masse, angrier than ever.

"Been there, done that," said my reader in a tone of assumed boredom.

"Yeah, said Socrates, "but this is no video game or no movie neither. This is for real. They are ghosts, all of them, the same as you or me. This city is the world's biggest magnet for ghosts. You know the song: New York, New York! Everyone wants a piece of the action. They want a genuine hunk of debris from the World Trade Center. Or maybe a salt shaker that looks like the Statue of Liberty. I used to have one of those, got it off a vendor down where we was docked. Five dollars. Other ghosts are no different. They're dead and they want to be part of the greatest crime scene in the world. Even before 9-11 it was a lot like this. Teeming: is that the word?"

"That's the word. And truly it's an amazing sight. But if it's all the same with you, Old Soc, I think I will switch channels." I slid my hand out from his waistband and waited for the horde around the taxi to wink out of existence, as it had when he'd run over one of the ghosts.

But they were still there in all their diversity, the starvelings and the obese hausfraus, the Aleuts and the Arabs in their burnooses and their burqas, the protesters and the junkies nodding out, zombie nuns and darling lost children having lots of fun. The whole family of man.

"Socrates," I said. "I still see them."

He nodded. "That's sometimes the trouble with alternate realities. Once you can see them it's hard to un-see them. But just turn your attention somewhere else, and they'll fade. We're almost at Alice's. Why don't *you* take the dog. Alice won't be able to see your friend here."

But when we got to Alice's address, she wasn't home. I rang and rang but no one answered. And there was no one at the entrance. Doormen were an extinct species, and the system of resident patrols that had replaced them were erratic and not to be trusted. As often as not *they* preyed upon one's visitors, not the other way around.

"It looks like you're stuck with me, fellow," I told Harry.

Harry barked his assent and gave me a reassuring lick

That was when we both saw Terror, standing near the taxi and swiveling his great T-Rex head in search of prey.

IX

Harry tried to break loose, and when I tightened the grip of my cradling arms, he nipped at my hand. Harry is small, but his nip is powerful. The first time Alice tried to lower him into her bathtub for a bath that nip sent her to the nearest Emergency Room for stitches in both her hands.

I needed no further persuasion. Harry was out of my arms—and into the fray. Instead of heading back from the field of battle or any otherwards than toward the enemy, like any dog of common sense, he ran right at him, yapping dog obscenities. Terror took a step back in sheer astonishment, as Goliath must have at his first sight of his puny challenger, indignant, as though to say, *This* is what they are sending against me! This midget!

Goliath lunged, David feinted, and then like any experienced martial artist facing a similar tactical dilemma he went for the giant's knees, digging his needlish teeth, straight into the nerve hard-wired to Maximum Pain. The huge dog reared up howling and then came down, crumpling forward on top of Harry. Harry eluded the raptor teeth and wriggled loose from underneath Terror's writhing bulk as he tried for a second bite.

It was not enough to have brought his enemy to the ground. Harry circled to the rear of him and what he'd done for his right foreleg he now did for his left hind leg. Terror howled again—the pain and the protest and the sheer disbelief united in a single chord. This time Harry held on, and

Terror seemed unable either to shake him off or to bite back. One crunch of his Godzilla jaws would have finished little Harry off, but with two legs crippled, and in a spastic haste, there was to be no coup de grace.

For a while I merely marveled at the contest, but then I realized that I must help Harry as Harry had helped me. Was the riddle knife still in my pocket? It was—and then it was in Terror's throat. He had no reproaches or astonishment left in him. He simply toppled to the sidewalk like an overturned building crane. There was an uncanny silence up and down the street. Blood makes no sound as it leaves a wound.

"Tom!" said Socrates, beckoning chauffeur-like by the opened car door. "Tom, I think we should go now. You too, Harry. Brave dog, yes you are."

Harry has a special way of walking, a kind of prance like a show horse , when he knows he's been especially good. After a disdainful sniff at the dying wolfhound, he pranced a victory prance back to the taxi, hopped in, and plunked down beside my reader, who pushed him away lest he get some of Terror's blood on his clothes.

X

People look back on the Twentieth Century as an age of innocence, a time when Terror didn't happen on a day-to-day basis, just individual rapes and murders, most of which never even made it to the Evening News. But the seeds of a darker era already existed back then. I remember being sent to Brazil by the U.S. State Department as an AmPart, an American Participant, to talk to Brazilian teens about science fiction, horror movies (*Terminator 2* had just come out, if you can think back that far), and abstinence. (Or maybe it was in Karachi that I talked about abstinence. In any case, it didn't seem to have much effect.) Most of the teens I talked to were herded into classrooms or auditoriums and were the usual mix of resentful, torpid, and eager to please as teens anywhere in the world. But one Sunday when I wasn't scheduled for anything (either in Sao Paolo or Brazilia) I went to a nearby boulevard or alameda where I'd been told it was the custom for teens to gather and groove to the sambas and suchlike being blasted out for the whole length of the street.

I'd imagined a polite orgy of flailing limbs and bottoms shaking like maracas, but what I found was a wide-screen version of *Dawn of the Dead*, a broad river of affectless, motionless, silent adolescents all wearing identical jeans and jackets of blue denim, the uniform of conformist poverty throughout the world, standing agaze while the lively, vapid music exhorted them to a cheerfulness they obviously wanted no part of. I took it as a portent of the world to come—and I was right for here they were again, those same zombies, now packed shoulder-to-shoulder and back to belly for the whole length and breadth of the immense tiered viewing platform of Footprint Lagoon, where once the World Trade Center had stood. The platform had spilled over into the promenade that continued on downtown as far as the South Ferry, and there too the undead of all ages stood looking to the west, toward that doleful icon of the post-9-11 era, the Statue of Liberty standing atilt, her face mutilated by a rocket's unlucky hit, her lifted arm torn from its socket, her torch doused by the polluted waters of the Hudson, which had risen to lap against Liberty's bronze toes. O say can you see, indeed!

Were there any living souls among this throng of silent sightseers? That's doubtful, for the area about Footprint Lagoon was considered unlucky and a likely source of contagion, especially for malaria. The few sightseers who still visited the Big Apple came to see a Disney musical or smoke a cigarette in Times Square, where tobacco was still legal. They never ventured this far downtown.

"I think, Socrates, if you don't mind…" I slipped my hand loose from his and watched the spectral throng slowly fade away, like cirrus dissolving in a high wind. The scene remained as cheerless as before, but cheerless in the grand romantic way of Byron's *Childe Harold*. "Unknelled, unto-kened, and unknown," and all that jazz.

"Don't you worry at all about the police?" my reader asked. "You did just kill a very large domestic animal and leave it bleeding in the street. There are surveillance cameras everywhere these days."

"Good thinking," said Socrates. "We should just leave the taxi where it's parked. It's not that far now to where the ferry leaves from."

I groaned in a subdued way.

"Now don't give me any of that arthritis shit, Tom. A bit of walking will do you good. Or maybe you'd like to have a bite to eat. I never see you eating a thing. It's unnatural, especially for a man of your..."

"I think the word you want is *girth*," my reader said.

"How do you maintain your girth, Tom, if you never eat? I mean, here I am, a ghost and yet if I don't get my ration of grog, or blood, or both, I just fade away."

"He has a theory," my reader said knowingly, "which was in one of his books about sci fi, that every long adventure story needs fuel stops at regular intervals for the characters to stop fighting the bad guys and loosen their belts and sit down and have a good dinner or at least a nice picnic."

"Stands to reason," said Socrates.

"I'm sorry," I said, "but I didn't pack a picnic."

"And it doesn't look like any of them did either," Socrates said, indicating the throngs lined up along the promenade staring blankly across the Hudson at the Jersey docks and high-rises.

"How did they get here in the first place?" I wondered aloud. "They seem so listless. I can't imagine any of them saying, 'Hey, why don't we head to New York City so we can look at the buildings that haven't been blown up yet.' Not that lot."

"I think they're blown here by the wind," said my reader. "Like spores. But not just any wind. More like a cyclone, or a whirlpool, or the drain in a bathtub. The wind of History, you might say. Actually you did say it, I'm just quoting."

"But you aren't hungry?" Socrates insisted.

"I'm tired. That can be a form of hunger, I guess. But there are no restaurants around here, Socrates, and even if there were, we couldn't bring Harry in with us. I wouldn't mind, however, if we sat down for a bit. On the grass somewhere?"

Socrates and my reader exchanged a significant look. "I guess now is as good a time as any," my reader said. "But it's not my job. *You* tell him."

"Tom, there is something you are not aware of. We thought you'd figure it out yourself. You know in Greece we have a saying, *Know thyself*. Damn, I don't know how to say this…"

"Just blurt it out, Socrates."

"Tom, you're like all the other people here. You're like me."

"Well, of course, Socrates. Just because I've published a few books doesn't mean I'm Superman or something."

"What he's trying to tell you, Mr. Disch," my reader burst out in a tone of exasperation, "is that you are dead."

XI

"Did I faint again?" I asked Socrates, raising my hand to prevent another slap across my face.

"Dead away, mate. I had to smack you, shaking didn't seem to help."

"I can't quite believe that a person can die without realizing it."

"People die in their sleep, don't they?" my reader reasoned.

"Is that what happened to me—I died in my sleep? And when? Last night? Or…?"

"A while before that, Tom."

"Before you sailed on the *Proteus*, Mr. Disch," my reader volunteered, eager to have a role in the denouement. "You died in the very same blue recliner that you returned from Greece in. Isn't that amazing!"

"Was it a heart attack?"

Socrates shook his head. "You were murdered—with the same knife you used on me. The murderer must have seen it on your desk."

"The bronze letter-opener you just used to kill that monstrous dog," said my reader. "I have one just like it. It's from the Metropolitan Museum gift shop. At least mine is."

"But then someone used it to kill Elizabeth Ashley."

"After it returned home with you."

"But who?"

"The same damned someone who killed you, Tom. Her brother."

"Aristotle?"

"Think about it, Tom."

I thought about it. Of course, the Ellises had a good, traditional motive. They wanted me out of my rent-subsidized apartment. During the whole year after the fire Aristotle had shillied and shallied and given one reason after another why it was taking so long to make the apartment habitable again, even though Ashley was back in her place inside of a few months. We spent a year exiled to the boonies. He figured he'd wear us down, and then when Charlie died as a side-effect of that exile, he figured I'd be worn down by the eviction proceedings. (And, insult to injury, our absence became part of his legal case for the eviction: we had not been on the premises for such a long while.) So he might have tried murder. I would not have been the first New York City tenant to be eased out of his apartment with the blade of a knife. It happens all the time on *Law and Order*.

So much for motive. As to opportunity, though they denied it, the Ellises had keys that accessed all the apartments in the building. If I'd been lying in a drowse in that blue recliner and if someone were to tiptoe in, slit my throat, and leave me there to bleed to death, how would I have known? But then there were riddles beyond that, not least of which concerned the riddle-knife itself. My murderer could not have thought to frame me for Ashley's death if I'd been killed first—and with the same weapon.

No, it simply made no sense, and furthermore I refused to believe it. The power of denial is on a par with the power of faith. You might say they are reciprocals. I was not dead, whatever Socrates and my reader said. I might be living in the Valley of the Shadow but I had not my quietus made. I had goals and purposes, though at the moment I could not quite remember what they were, because once again I had fainted. Or maybe this whole last meditation was part of my original faint when I was told that

I was dead. There is a branch of philosophy that deals with just such questions. I think it's called epistemology.

XII

Invocation the Second

Memory, this one's for you. You are the Mother of the Muses, but it's them who always get the invocations. Yet it's you who are the source not just of each and every art but of human identity itself, for if we can't remember any of our yesterdays, how can we know who we have been or who we are right now? Maybe I'm more aware of my debt to Mnemosyne than most folks, since I have a trick memory, the way some have a trick knee. Once, some ten years ago or so, I opened a book I'd bought the day before at the Strand (I don't remember what it was) and I saw that though it was supposed to be new (albeit a remainder) there were notes in the margins. Curiosity won out over mere indignation, and I read what the commentator had written. It seemed both apposite to the text and deft in its phrasing. Only slowly did it dawn on me that I was that commentator, that the night before, after the Strand, when I was dining at Pizza Pizza (a restaurant that no longer exists, alas), I'd begun to read the book and to make notes in it. The notes were still there, but in my memory was no trace of what I'd read or what I'd written.

Blackouts like that are a common phenomenon for those who sometimes drink too much, but they also affect computers who are strict teetotalers. Once, in my lost Eden of Barryville, lightning struck close by the house and the computer I'd been working on, a Compaq, had its hard-drive fried.

Some of the files were later recovered by a tech, but others were lost irreversibly. At this point, I don't remember which files those may have been.

And that's the way with Memory. While she is with us she seems the essence of who we are, but let her slip from our sight, and she may be lost beyond recall. My own mother is a good for-instance. Up to the age of seventeen, when I left home, I must have had thousands and thousands of hours of conversation with my mother. She was a talker; we all are, we Disches. But what did we talk *about?* What opinions did she have about the news on the radio? About the doings (often reprehensible) of other Disches and Gilbertsons. My memory is as blank on that score as the hard-drive of that Compaq. I remember some of the books I read back then much better. Though maybe I only think I do. Recently I tried to re-read *The Return of the Native,* which I'd first read, with immense admiration, in the tenth grade. I admired it again on my second go-round, but no ember of memory was rekindled.

No, memory is a gift, and we must entreat it to visit us, as we would any of her daughters.

So, tell me, mother dearest, who am I, and what was done in those lost hours or last days of my life that I have so thoroughly forgotten?

XIII

"Tom," said Socrates in his most coaxing tone, quite as though he were talking to Harry, "do you think this is the right time to be on your feet walking about?"

"Yes, you can see for yourself it's getting dark. And besides—" Harry tugged at his leash with unexpected strength and urgency, and I stumbled once again, though it was not really a case of my losing my balance. Harry barked, urging me to get to my feet again, but for a little while I remained on my knees, enchanted by the coolness of the grass.

"Besides?" my reader prompted, as though the loss of a single train of thought was some kind of misdemeanor.

"Besides," I declared, "memory is not some kind of *muscle*. We can't just say, 'Memory, remember this, remember that.' It's more a knee-jerk sort of thing. It's cued by something happening now that brings us back to something else that happened back when. Just now, for instance, when I tried to stand up—That's what I've got to do, I've got to stand up."

I stood up without the least difficulty. It was amazing.

"Just now I remembered how, when we first moved to Union Square, it was at the nadir of its decline and the park had been surrendered to the junkies. They came there to score and stayed there to snore. Hey, that's pretty neat, isn't it, the rhyme? Anyhow, I remember—Harry, hold your horses!" He was pulling me southward, toward the ferry station, which was still a ways away.

"The thing is," I went on (but yielding to Harry's straining at the leash), "I can understand taking drugs to get high. But these guys were zombies. Sometimes they'd be standing in the middle of the street stopping the traffic and sort of tipping forward, swaying but never quite falling over. But not getting out of the way of the traffic either. I swear I had to go and lead them to the sidewalk by the hand (I wonder if that's where 'main force' comes from?), and I'd leave them there, still tipping over and swaying.

"Tuenol, that was the name of the drug they were taking. I guess it was some kind of tranquilizer, but they were beyond tranquil. They were zombies."

"Like the people today, looking across the river—is that what you're saying?"

"That's what *you're* saying, but yeah, like them. And now I finally understand what they saw in their Tuenol."

"Death!" my reader declared, as one who'd just announced a winning Bingo card.

"In a way, yes. What they saw was a world from which the future had been erased. And it's the same world those people today could see across the river. In the west."

"Oh, yes, you were always a big one on Spengler. But Mr. Disch, you certainly have learned by now that Spengler is, how shall we say, a disreputable taste."

"Yeah?" said Socrates. "Now you're talking my language. You see that guy over there behind the monument that looks like a big pineapple? He's been sending signals for at least three minutes. Not that I've got a stopwatch but you understand. You two head on to the ferry house, I'll catch up."

I let Harry have his way with me, and while we heading for the ferries' dock I went on expounding my theory of Tuenol, the Death Wish, and the end of western civilization.

"Mr. Disch," said my reader, as we drew near the ticket booth inside the dimly lighted lobby, "that was all *very* interesting. But we have been together the whole day now, and the fact is I am *terrified* of water. Of being on a boat that's on the water, or even going over a bridge. So if you don't mind, I must excuse myself." With which he disappeared like a light bulb that's been turned off.

"Harry, old pal, it looks like it's just you and me now."

Harry barked to say that that was all right with him.

XIV

I was sure from the way the guy in the ticket booth was eying Harry that he was going to give us grief. As we drew nearer the counter he raised himself up from his stool so he could look down at my companion. "What kind of dog is that?" he asked. People often ask. Lhasa apsos are not a common breed, even in sophisticated New York. Also (Alice tells me) dogs are not as common on the streets these days as once they were, where dognapping has become almost as common as kidnapping. They are considered money on a leash.

When I explained that he was a lhasa apso, a Tibetan breed, and that his name was Harry, the fellow a smiled a rather sinister smile (can one smile in any other wise when one has a pencil-line mustache?) and asked, "And he's a fighter, is he?"

"Yes, indeed. You should have seen him in action this morning. A regular little Mike Tyson."

Knowing himself to be the subject of our admiration, Harry lifted his rump off the marble floor so he could wag his tail and gave a short bark of acknowledgment.

"Here," the ticket vendor said, handing me a small numbered tag (34), "put this on his collar. And for you.... Gimme your hand." I slid my hand through the slot cut in the thick green-tinged glass and he stamped it with a rubber stamp that left a vivid purple proof of admission right above my knuckles: U.S. TROPE.

"It's an anagram," I marveled.

"I wouldn't know about that. It's the name of the boat. Ferries are named after politicans mostly. There's the Molinari, the Gotti. I don't know who this Trope was or any of the rest of them, except Gotti. Anyhow you have a good time, the both of you. I'll be rooting for ya. But remember, don't let him off the leash inside there." He flashed me a sideways V with his left hand and then began to deal with the next person in line.

The ferry was already in the slip, so there was no need to wait in the terminal, which had been much expanded and spruced up since the last time I'd been on the ferry. Which would have been when? I'd no idea. I'd only ever been on the ferry for the sake of the ferry ride itself. In those days it was the poor man's air conditioner. For five cents you could spend an hour in Oahu.

Cars drove on to the ferry at street level; but pedestrians had to go one floor up, so I scooped Harry up and mounted the escalator, then carried him across the big steel gangplank onto the boat. It felt like stepping into another century, a past at least as long ago as ancient Greece. Once on deck I managed to get the No. 34 tag on Harry's collar. He fidgeted but suffered the deed to be done. "Good dog," I told him.

Once we were inside the big barn of the passenger cabin with its aisles and rows of dark wooden benches, I let Harry lead me where he would. He was in an entirely novel smell-world and he moved from one astonishing odor to the next like a drunken vacuum cleaner. Sometimes he would come upon another of his own kind, but there was no chance to strike up an acquaintance for all the other dogs were pent up inside cages or carriers of heavy-duty mesh. Poor creatures (I thought), lucky Harry.

At last Harry came to where he knew he had to be, and he parked himself in front of a woman in the middle of the cabin with an air of Here-stand-I finality.

I was totally taken aback, for the woman seated on the bench before him, with a basket full of single-shot bottles of liquor and bags of potato chips, was my own mother. Not as I remembered her but as she would have been if she'd survived her cancer and lived another twenty years.

And then I realized that no, that wasn't who this woman was at all. She was my old friend from ancient Greece, Cassandra, pythoness and princess of Troy, now a gap-toothed crone with snarly gray hair, who asked me, in a snarly voice, "Whadaya want?"

And though I'd called on Mnemosyne only moments earlier to come to my assistance, the only answer I could think of was "Anything but you, sweetheart. Anything but you."

XV

I was too well-bred to say something so black-hearted to an old lady selling booze from a canvas tote. I just stood there, struck dumb, staring.

Cassandra said, "The chips are a buck, the rum is five. I also got sandwiches. Ham or cheese. They're ten. Pay in advance."

"Cassandra?"

"Yeah, that's my name. What's yours? Do I know you?"

"I'm Tom."

"Well, I've met a lot of Toms in my day. But you look wrecked. Why not sit down here a bit and tell me where you think we met. And have one of these." She dug into her tote and took out a mini of Bacardi. "On the house." I took it as one might accept hospitality from one of the shades in hell. The woman was my mother's identical twin and the clone of the Cassandra I had known. And both resemblances seemed coincidental. Because primarily she seemed to be just the old slag she was.

I sat where she'd invited me to sit, looking dumbly at the little bottle in my hand. When I made no effort to open it, she took it from my hand, twisted the cap off, and replaced it in my hand. "Skol!"

I raised the bottle to my lips, took the smallest sip, and felt the warmth of the liquor rush through me like a sniff of smelling salts.

"Have you ever been to Greece, Cassandra?"

She laughed. "Do I look like someone who's ever been to Greece?"

"You look like someone I knew there at one time. But I guess that's ancient history now."

"Drink!" she urged, and when I obeyed, she said, "Here's the deal. I can't legally sell food on the boat. Never mind the boat itself is not exactly legal. Leastways, not today. But I can offer an artistic product for sale. Which means I can do your portrait,"

"God, that would be the last thing I want."

"I know what you mean, Tom. But do you want a cheese sandwich or don't you?"

I checked my wallet. I gave her the one bill I had left.

"Where *are* you from, Cassandra?"

"These days, Staten Island. But for most of my life San Diego. The fire changed all that."

"Your home burned down?"

"Not exactly. But the state did. Could you turn your head more sideways, towards me? What I mean is San Diego is part of Mexico now. And it's not a safe place for people like us. Not that Staten Island is a whole lot better. The country is falling to pieces, haven't you noticed? Now stop talking for a minute or so so I can draw you. You've got such a blah face. Nothing really distinctive. That's the hardest kind to draw. Listen to the music."

There was no music. "There is no music," I told her.

"Listen harder." She went on sketching and finally turned the tablet around to show me a workaday but recognizable charcoal head-and-shoulders sketch of Socrates, not as I'd seen him in the course of our day together but as he might appear some miles down the road. What was the word she had used when she'd invited to sit beside her? Wrecked.

XVI

Oh dear, I thought. That can't be. I looked about the broad, low cabin for a mirror just to be sure it couldn't be. Not a mirror in sight. But I knew where I could find one. "Excuse me," I said to Cassandra. "Would you look after Harry for just a minute? I have to go to the men's room." I handed the leash to Cassandra.

She scowled, and then grinned letting me have a full view of her dental misfortunes. "What Harry?" she asked.

And indeed at the other end of the leash there was no Harry. My knot had untied itself, as so often my knots do. I have a pair of slippers that will not hold the knot in their stiff leather- thong ties from one side of the room to the other. I was exasperated at his running off, but getting to a mirror was still my first priority.

"He must have gone to find his own doggy men's room. He'll be back. Maybe you can give him a nibble from that sandwich I bought but still haven't seen. Okay?"

"Okay, but you better hurry, Mister. The fights are going to start any minute. Things can get rowdy on the deck below, and that's where the head is. Men downstairs, women up here, that's the rule."

As though on cue a gong sounded, and a loud (albeit muted) cheer went up. A sports cheer, with that special edge of homicidal bonhomie that is reserved for events that promise the sight of spilled blood.

I hurried down a flight of steps to where, usually, the cars are parked. But there were few cars on board for this trip, and those formed a kind of barricade in the forward part of the deck, beyond which, facing away from me in the same direction as the cars, a crowd had gathered, huddled down but restless. An amplified voice announced: "Number Twenty-Eight. Butterblood. Breed: unknown."

That cheer again. A few voices calling out their encouragement: "Go for it, Butterblood!" "Tear him to pieces!" "Muerto! Muerto!"

"Number Thirty-Four. Mike Tyson. Breed: Lhasa apso."

Another cheer, mixed with ill-intending laughter. The same voice that had bidden Butterblood to go for it, called out, "Watch out, Butterblood—Mike is known to *bite*."

I made my way forward, across the dark, oil-stained steel plates of the deck toward where the viewers were assembled. I heard a low growl, then a sound for which the language has no name, and a howl of pain. It was Harry's howl, and there would be many more, one after another, but from Butterblood only the sound of his attack.

As for the crowd, I think those who gathered to watch the scourging and crucifixion may have sounded much the same. Blood-lust makes all men equal. Boisterous, hyperventilated, hungry to see worse, ears to be torn off, eyes gouged, the anguish of assaulted innocence. I did not go any closer. I could not bear to watch poor Harry torn to pieces. I knew I could not stop the fight.

When it was over and the fans turned their attention to settling their wagers, I went forward to try to collect my darling's body, but one of the fight attendants, an overweight teenager with grungy blond dreadlocks, waved me away. "The dead ones go over the side," he explained. "We don't want any evidence around."

So I watched while the boy used a push-broom to nudge Harry's corpse, a few inches at a time, across the steel deck and over the edge into the polluted waters of the sound.

XVII

"Please have a seat, Mr. Disch," said the doctor, and then without waiting for me to do so:

"And how are we today?"

"We?" I wondered. If ever there were a situation where "we" would seem the wrong pronoun surely it is a doctor's office. Do prison guards and wardens address their charges as "we"? At least, I was "Mr. Disch" and not "Tom."

"And have we had our meds today?"

"Yes, Doctor," said Nurse Protoplast, who was standing behind me, with ball-point and notepad on the ready. "And I checked to be sure he swallowed them. This time."

Her name was not really Protoplast. I just called her that in homage to the *Proteus*. We'd been shipmates aboard the *Proteus*, she and I, in times gone by. Whereas the doctor was a much more recent acquaintance. I'd known him only as "my reader" on my last day of liberty in the city.

"Good. Then I expect he no longer believes himself to be a Greek god!!"

"I never supposed that, Doctor."

"And those friends of yours, Socrates and Aga-ding-dong? They weren't gods either?"

And this was the man who was looking after *my* mental health! But I had to remember he was *trying* to get a rise out of me.

"I think I've already explained, Sir, who they were, and the nature of our connection."

He gave a grimace of satisfaction. "Yes. They were your hallucinations. Brought into being by the trauma of your eviction."

"And are you any otherwise?" I wanted to ask him. But I knew better than to try. He might send me right back to the violent ward.

"They were my hallucinations," I agreed. "Like the dog. Like the ferryboat."

"But you did try to jump from the ferry," the doctor pointed out.

I had no memory of that at all, but it seemed like a reasonable thing to do, and I am prone to memory blackouts. In the circumstances. I could feel the tears welling up, though, at the memory of Harry. He was such a good dog. And I knew he'd been no hallucination.

I could see he was waiting for my answer, so I hastened to say, "Yes, that was a foolish thing to do. We must always be grateful for the gift of life. Even when things aren't going just our way. That's when we've got to say, Hey, I'm lucky just to be alive."

"Well, you've certainly got that down pat, Tom."

Tom! There it was. A breakthrough in our anti-relationship.

"Isn't that what *you* believe, doctor?"

He ignored my little dig. "If you were to be sent to a halfway house, Tom, somewhere *not* in Manhattan, would you be able to promise me to observe a few simple rules?"

I nodded a serious, solemn nod. "Take our pills. Attend our meetings. Look on the bright side. Right."

"And also, Tom, you must agree *not* to return to your old address, *not* to try and telephone Aristotle Ellis, or his sisters, or Elizabeth Ashley. She finds your calls particularly distressing."

"She should."

The doctor modulated his tone to one of professional sympathy. "And why is that, Tom?"

I tried to think of something so smarmy he could not gainsay it. "Did that seem unfriendly of me? Or bitter? I hope not. Elizabeth is a lovely person. At heart."

He sighed. "Well, your case has been up for review again, and I will be honest with you, Tom. *I* was not in favor of your release. Not at all. I *dread* to think what you may do when you are back on the street. As soon as you're out of here I am sure you will be off your meds and back in ancient Greece, or whatever port your *Proteus* is bound for next. I believe you are incorrigible. But the decision does not rest with me. Are his papers in order, nurse?"

"They are, doctor.

He pushed his chair back and stood up. He didn't offer his hand to be shaken, and neither did I.

At the door the nurse offered me a shopping bag with all my possessions and a folder full of documents testifying to my release. In high school it had been much the same. I'd graduated, but there was not to be a ceremony. I guess there might have been if I'd bothered going to it. It wasn't that I hadn't been happy to be done with the long ordeal. I was, very. And now it was the same again. When I'd exited the lobby and could see the blue sky of heaven I felt a sense of relief that was almost like elation. I had reached my own personal end of the world. I was free.

Any questions?